George Chatt

Miscellaneous Poems

George Chatt

Miscellaneous Poems

ISBN/EAN: 9783337397739

Printed in Europe, USA, Canada, Australia, Japan

Cover: Foto ©Andreas Hilbeck / pixelio.de

More available books at **www.hansebooks.com**

MISCELLANEOUS POEMS.

BY

GEORGE CHATT.

HEXHAM:

PRINTED AT THE COURANT OFFICE, BY J. CATHERALL & CO.

—

1866.

INDEX.

PREFACE.

Such of the public as may favour me with a perusal
of these trifles should be informed that they are not the
laboured efforts of a well-cultured mind, learned in the
wisdom of the schools, and possessing all the appliances
for careful study, but the productions of a farm labourer,
in the few scattered hours of leisure snatched from a
toilsome occupation; therefore I hope the critical eye
will scan their imperfections charitably, and, where merit
is discovered, that his approbation may not be withheld.

Several of the poems which make up this little
volume have already been published in the columns of
the local newspapers, mostly in the *Hexham Courant;*
to the editor of that flourishing publication I am greatly
indebted for kind encouragement and advice in this
project.

It would be an insult to the taste of my numerous
subscribers and to those gentlemen, eminent among the
northern *literati*, who have given favourable opinions of
my published productions, to affect an ignorance of any
merit they may contain; yet the critic will have little
difficulty in finding weak passages, and, if I dare presume to anticipate his verdict, he will be likely to con-

demn the sentiments comprised in some of the pieces, and censure the bad taste that should allow me sometimes to obtrude my own troubles upon a happy world, which can receive no possible interest from their recital. These poems were nearly all written in the intervals between weeks of dull, continuous labour, which tended to depress the mind, and force out those gloomy emanations that might be mistaken for the pitiful whinings of egotism, or the inventions of a bard's weak fancy, who, for the lack of other ideas, wove them in to give effect to his strain.

But, alas! I am no silken poet, reared among comforts, and rejoicing in the advantages of superior education, who has been crammed with all the choice dainties of ancient and modern lore, and without a care on his mind to disturb the train of his glowing ideas. The little volume here offered to the discriminating public is the work of one who in infancy was initiated to hard labour, and whose youth was passed in discouraging servitude; if his work is approved by the public it will give him the highest gratification, but if it bears no claim to that approval, let him receive the contempt which his presumption deserves.

G. C.

DEDICATION

TO

SIR ROWLAND STANLEY ERRINGTON, BART.,

OF

SANDHOE HOUSE, NORTHUMBERLAND.

———◆——

SIR, the poor bard who here presents his lays,
Ne'er courted favour by mean gifts of praise;
The phrases trite that serv'd each previous age,
Shall not appear upon my truthful page;
And he, who deign'd kind notice to bestow
On one in social grade obscure and low,
Alike would empty compliments despise,
That please the foolish but disgust the wise;
Yet men admiring tell his virtues o'er,—
They will exalt his memory evermore,—
The open hand that doth the needy fill,
The genial heart that loves to spread goodwill,
The courteous mien by honour dignified;
These make his name revered throughout Tyneside.

As for the bard, thus far his path has been
Where no kind ray illumed life's barren scene;
Born amid toil, and bred in servitude,
With phrase unpolished and demeanour rude,

He yet doth own a spirit that would fain
Burst forth to light and break the servile chain;
But dull dependence drags the soul to earth,
Each soaring thought is stifled in its birth;
And flickering faint beneath the adverse blast,
The fire of genius pales, and dies at last.
Yet would not I presume high gifts to claim,
Or dare to think my works would merit fame;
Unwont am I on mystic tomes to pore,
Unknown to me is schoolmen's valued lore;
The book of nature I have learnt to spell,
Life's varied phases I have noted well;
Therefore my rhymes are simple, plain, and true,
Nor thus contemn'd when countenanced by you.

Accept the thanks a humble poet gives,
In whom a grateful sense of favour lives.
On you and yours may lasting peace abide,
And vice abash'd far from your presence hide;
That all your actions still may tend to cause
Heaven's high approval and the world's applause;
In calm enjoyment of all plenty rest,
Till call'd at last to Heaven's fruition blest.

I have the honour to be, Sir,
Your obedient Servant,

GEORGE CHATT.

Eastland Bank, Hexham,
April 17th, 1866.

Bonnie Tyneside.

OH, bonnie Tyneside ! I shall see it once more,
   After long years of exile away from its shore :
Through far foreign countries a rambler I've been,
And much have I suffer'd, and much have I seen ;
And I've lived in lands where a brighter sun shone,
Yet ne'er saw a country so fair as my own ;
And I never have seen, in my wanderings wide,
A spot I loved better than bonnie Tyneside.

Oh, bonnie Tyneside ! where my infancy pass'd,
Like a beautiful dream, too happy to last ;
Oh, I'll see the bright hills where in childhood we strayed,
And the school green at Wall where so often we've played ;
And the schoolmaster still at the village is seen,
And the school children still are at play on the green ;
But the class-mates I knew they are gone far and wide,
They have wander'd away from bonnie Tyneside.

Oh, bonnie Tyneside ! I come weary and worn,
How few are the friends left to greet my return !
I'll away to the hills, and I'll wander all day,
Along the green banks where the lambs are at play ;
Oh, the poor silly sheep know their tracks o'er the fell !
And the bonnie wee birds have a home in the dell ;
But a home and a hearth I have yet to provide,
For I am a stranger to bonnie Tyneside.

Oh, bonnie Tyneside ! my darling is there ;
She waits for my coming her love to declare ;
Since the day that we parted she faithful has been.
Though the wide ocean lay like a barrier between ;
Oh, she's fair as the morning of beautiful May,
And bright as the eve of a midsummer day ;
How happy I'd be with her for my bride,
In a snug little cottage in bonnie Tyneside.

Where should my Dwelling be.

WHERE should my dwelling be ?
      Not 'mid the scenes of struggling life ;
Not in the city's war and strife ;
Where misery and misfortune haunt,
With tyrant Wealth and slavish Want,
      And Mammon's rule we see.
But I would dwell in solitude,
Where wasting care might not intrude ;
Secure would be my lonely fate,
From friends who envy, foes who hate.

      How should my life be spent ?
Not in the greedy quest for gold,
Eager to have what others hold ;
Let sordid minds endanger health,
Or risk their souls in seeking wealth,
      Or pine in discontent.

Give me but wherewithal to live,
Peace and a pure conscience give :
Then keep your wealth in many a heap,
Your pride and costly luxuries keep.

Where should my form be laid,
When I am dead to earthly pains ?
Not with the great in gilded fanes ;
Not in the crowded graveyard—no ;
But in the quiet vale below,
    And just within the glade.
And they should write above my head,
Not empty flatteries for the dead,
But words affectionate and true,
By friendship given, warm and few.

The Soldier's Burial.

GREAT Gib-el-Tarif* throws its shade
    Across the graveyard wide ;
'Twas there our comrade's form we laid
    At balmy eventide.

The "Dead March" echoes from the hill,
    In sweetly mournful strains ;
All else around is deathly still,
    A solemn silence reigns.

* Gib-el-Tarif, i.e., Rock of Tarif, the name given to Gibraltar by the Moors.

The zephyrs waft a sweet perfume
From many a balmy grove ;
The orange sheds its fragrant bloom
Where happy lovers rove.

The setting sun yet brightly shines
On mountain summits gray,
And underneath the spreading vines
The laughing children play.

The ships departing o'er the seas
Move slow, with hanging sails
Scarce ruffled by the gentle breeze
From Andalusia's vales.

The Funeral March is ringing still,
Like wailing spirits near ;
And eyes which pity seldom fill,
Now drop the melting tear.

At length within their narrow home
His cold remains are laid,
And " Dust to dust," in solemn tone,
By reverend lips is said.

The mother's hope, the father's pride,
He sleeps on yonder shore ;
Their cottage stands by Coquetside,
Where he'll return no more.

A comrade kind, a soldier brave,
Who knew him best can tell ;
Three volleys fire o'er his grave,
He served his country well.

On Board the Petrel.

OH, happy were we, happy were we,
  The Petrel's merry crew ;
As o'er the sea, the bright blue sea,
  Our brave barque onward flew.
We sailed by many a pleasant shore—
  Round many a sunny isle,
Where the sweet balm and spices are,
  And Spring doth ever smile.

We were a blythe and joyous crew,
  And stalwart every one,
Each at the trial-time true-blue,
  A craven traitor none.
We loved the sea, the open sea,
  Where bold the billows ran,
For there we felt secure and free
  From the wiles of cunning man.

And when the midnight storm awoke,
  Its warfare wild to wage,
I've smiled as forth its fury broke,
  And laughed, ha ! ha ! at its rage.
For better it is the storm to meet,
  Though fierce and fell it seems,
Than face the treacherous world's deceit—
  Man's many trickful schemes.

And when we reach'd the busy port,
　　Then did the bright gold fly,
Then in a whirl of joyous sport,
　　The days and nights flew by.
And when at last our money fail'd,
　　We went on board again ;
Up anchor, ho ! and away we sail'd
　　Across the stormy main.

But fierce the winter tempest blew
　　On Barbary's rugged coast ;
Mast high the spray in showers flew,
　　And our gallant barque was lost.
And half our noble crew sank deep
　　'Neath ocean's troubled breast,
Brave hearts that now in silence sleep,
　　With the mighty dead at rest.

The remnant of the Petrel's crew
　　Resought Old England's shore,
And there with many a fond adieu
　　We parted evermore.
But ye shall ne'er forgotten be,
　　My messmates kind and true ;
For happy were we, happy were we,
　　The Petrel's merry crew.

Aim Higher.

AIM higher ! let thy genius soar
  On heaven directed wings ;
Earth's hollow vanities abhor,
  Esteem not worldly things ;
Blind Folly's crowded path eschew,
But walk with Wisdom's light in view,
  On wide domains of Art ;
New regions in that land explore,
And bring fresh beauties from its shore,
  To cheer each drooping heart.

Aim higher ! though the worldling's sneer
  Assail at every turn ;
Thou in the vanguard shall appear,
  Despite his withering scorn,
The pamper'd progeny of Pride,
By showy raiment dignified,
  May strut disdainful by :
Yet when their little day is o'er,
Their proud names shall be heard no more,
  But thine shall never die.

Aim higher ! rise amid the crowd
  Of cares which weigh thee down :
Dull Ignorance may clamour loud,
  And Pride impotent frown ;

And Envy gnaw its spiteful tongue,
And all the vain and vaunting throng
 Around thy footsteps rave ;
The shallow brood of Emptiness
Across thy upward path may press,
 Yet forward with the brave.

Aim higher ! reach the fairest spot
 Where Truth eternal reigns ;
Bright treasures from that realm are got,
 Yet brighter there remains.
Go, gather gems of priceless worth,
To bless, to benefit the earth,
 While countless crowds acclaim.
Then after toils and struggles hard,
Thy work shall have its sweet reward :
 So higher be thy aim.

November Winds.

NOVEMBER winds, that wildly sweep
 Around my dwelling lone ;
And at its uncouth gable keep
 A sad and plaintive moan :
I love to hear—at midnight drear—
 That weird and mournful tone.

The churlish blast drives o'er the fell,
  Where erst the lark was heard,
And down the dark, dismantled dell,
  Where late the zephyr stirr'd,
Through fields forlorn, where waved the corn,
  Where roved the bee and bird.

Earth's summer beauties all are gone,
  Its autumn glories fled ;
The flowers are faded every one,
  Their gorgeous bloom is dead ;
The sunshine bright hath left our sight,
  And winter reigns instead.

And now I sit, and muse alone,
  While loud the winds do blow,
On evanescent pleasures gone,
  Like summer's fleeting glow,
On dreams that fade, and hopes decayed,
  Though cherish'd long ago.

King Alcohol.

OH, mighty king ! whose potent sway
 Millions in every land obey ;
In every town thy vassals meet :
Thy court is held in every street,
Where the frantic throng flock night and day,
And with bestial rites their fealty pay ;
They blindly yield to thy harsh control,
Thy willing slaves, King Alcohol.

All ranks of men to thy courts repair,
Seeking unhallowed pleasures there—
Delusive pleasures, that end in pain,
That weaken the mind and warp the brain.
Fill, fill the glass and look therein,
See the chief source of sorrow and sin ;
All vices lurk in thy witching bowl,
That darken the earth, King Alcohol.

How are thy subjects ruled by thee ?
Thou givest a moment's maudlin glee ;
The feeble soul awhile is brave,
And the empty braggart loud doth rave,
And the vacant laugh is heard between
The senseless song and the jest obscene :
Till thy maddened votaries helpless roll
Beneath thy feet, King Alcohol.

What bounties, what rewards have they,
Who grovel thus to thy tyrant sway ?
Thou givest every rankling woe,
This vice-accursed world doth know,
And all the griefs and burning pains,
That sin hath caused, that hell contains.
The tortured body and troubled soul,
Thou givest to them, King Alcohol.

Let not the wine cup's witching smile
Thy sober thoughts and sense beguile ;
Oh, false the spirit the drunkard hires,
And hollow the mirth which wine inspires.
But the glorious day is drawing near,
When the curse from the land will disappear ;
And the groaning earth will end its dole,
When thy reign shall cease, King Alcohol.

The Dream.

IN a dream of the night, I was roaming far,
    Through a strange and a shadowy land ;
And I sought the shore where the dark waves roar,
    As they rush on the rocky strand.
The sun had shrunk in the lurid sky,
    And pale was the light on earth it shed—
The wide earth which lay in its twilight ray,
    Like the drear abode of the silent dead.

'Tis fearful to wander alone, alone,
　　On dreamland's dim and silent shore—
To wander alone, where joy is unknown,
　　And solitude reigns for evermore.
But I heard soft music floating by,
　　Sad as the sound of the surging sea,
Mournful as love-sick maiden's sigh,
　　And sweet as seraph-tun'd harp could be.

And I felt a soothing influence near,
　　When lo, in the ray of a brighter land,
I saw a beauteous form appear,
　　On rainbow glories it seemed to stand.
" 'Tis she ; I know those heaven-bright eyes—
　　That form in angel grace arrayed ;
My life is wasting away in sighs—
　　In longing sighs for thee, sweet maid.

" Oh ! let me come to those beauteous arms,
　　To live a moment there and die ;
Let me but breathe where thy beauty charms,
　　No dearer wish on earth have I."
And a brighter smile did her eyes illume,
　　Than ever the face of the morning wore ;
Then slow she vanish'd amid the gloom,
　　And I saw her heavenly form no more.

And I, my desolate path I trac'd
　　Over rugged mountains and valleys bare ;
And the bleak winds moan'd through the dreary waste,
　　Like the wail of a soul in lost despair.

Yet that heavenly smile doth cheer me still,
   Through long, long years of the bitterest woe;
Oh, life would be joyless, dark, and chill,
   But for the love born long ago.

Away on the Hills.

AWAY on the hills, I love to roam,
   Where the winter-swollen streamlets foam ;
Where the furious winds rush madly past,
And the dark pines bend to the shrieking blast ;
Where the curlew screams in its wild retreat,
And the fleet hare bounds from its lowly seat ;
Where the moor fowl crouch on their heathery bed,
And the restless plover wails overhead,
Oh my heart leaps free, unfettered then,
Away from the crowded haunts of men.

   Away on the hills, I love to stray,
On the quiet morn of a Sabbath day ;
When the sunbeams bright on their summits glow,
And the white mists sleep in the vale below ;
When the silvery chimes of the distant bells
Come softened over the sunlit fells ;
When the lark springs up in the summer sky,
To warble its soothing song on high.
Oh, here, where His wondrous works appear,

Lift up thy heart in devotion here.
No frivolous forms, nor rites we need,
By man ordained to suit a creed ;
No lengthened prayers, nor preachings vain,
To shroud the truth of the Scripture plain ;
But with humble hope, and faith sincere,
Lift up thy heart in devotion here.

Away on the hills, I love to stray,
Where the blithe birds sing all the summer day ;
Where toil's rude clang doth never intrude
In the midst of their quiet solitude ;
Where a master's frown evokes no fear,
And his harsh commands are impotent here.
Here let thy spirit crush'd by toil,
Leap gladly free from its yoke servile,
And soar in the track of the mountain bird,
Where the world's mad clamour is never heard,
Where the lark, sweet bird, its glad song trills,
Away on the hills, the free, bright hills.

Banks of the Tyne.

OH, the winter winds sweep over waste-heath and wild-wood,
 And plaintively moan at my window all day ;
And the beautiful scenes where I dreamt away childhood
 Look sombre and sad in their winter array.
Oh, scenes of my childhood ! delighted I ponder
 On days when the sweets of enjoyment were mine,
Through the summer-clad fields in the evening to wander,
 Or the green groves adorning the Banks of the Tyne.

Then to muse on the dark days of rapine and murder,
 When our forefathers followed the freebooters' trade ;
Bold bands of moss-troopers swept over the Border,
 And made the stout hearts of our dalesmen afraid.
But the reiver is seen in our valleys no longer,
 Where the pathway of Progress refulgent doth shine ;
No more must the weaker succumb to the stronger,
 Secure in our laws on the Banks of the Tyne.

I have strayed on the margin of many a river,
 And roam'd in the countries away o'er the sea,
In the sweet orange groves near the bright Guadalquiver,
 Yet the land of my birth is the dearest to me.
And pleasant it is on the balm-laden morning,
 With the passion-swayed girls of the South 'neath the vine
Yet they lack the soft graces our own maids adorning—
 The fresh bloom they wear on the Banks of the Tyne.

Though fortune is harsh, yet wherever sojourning,
    Unheeding the cares weighing heavily down,
The glitter and glare of the hollow world scorning,
    I can laugh in defiance at Fate's darkest frown.
And man, I have studied thy innermost nature,
    Like a difficult volume deep line after line ;
Oh world, I've discovered thy darkness of feature,
    While battling thee far from the Banks of the Tyne.

Let the venal bard, nurst in the soft lap of pleasure,
    At Mammon's behest all his powers awake ;
The world may applaud his effeminate measure,
    But the meed which he covets I would not partake ;
Though its strains may lack sweetness, let Truth tune my lyre,
    Then shall Virtue triumphant the laurel-wreath twine ;
And with ardent thoughts kindled at Nature's own fire,
    I'll weave my rude song on the Banks of the Tyne.

In the bright days of childhood life's pathway was pleasant,
    No shadow of care on its radiance fell ;
Then let Hope with its halo encircle the present,
    And smile in the future, its gloom to dispel.
No more of the evils that darken existence,
    Let cheerful content amid deep troubles shine ;
Lo, happiness looms in the far-away distance,
    With love's sweet delights on the Banks of the Tyne.

——o——

Dreamland.

IN Sleep's delightful realm, the soul doth wander
   On happy shores where gorgeous sunbeams glow ;
Where crystal streams through summer vales meander,
   And flowers of rarest hues their perfume throw.

The rills, that murmur through the groves enchanted,
   Sound like the echo of low music hush'd ;
By seraph songs the ambient air is haunted,
   As though the strains from Heaven's own portal gush'd.

A sweet Elysian peace, that earthward falling
   Like softest dew, pervades all nature there ;
The green woods listen to the birds carolling,
   No discord rude disturbs the tranquil air.

Each thing partaking sentient life rejoices,
   There is no source of grief, no cause of woe ;
We see bright forms, and hear angelic voices,
   Long lost, that charm'd the rapt soul long ago.

Far off, I see another Eden shining,
   Where two fond hearts exist in concord calm ;
Two kindred souls in bliss ecstatic joining,
   Whose lives are steep'd in love's delicious balm.

Oh, Love ! thou dost life's weary burden lighten,
   Thy cheerful smile dispels dull care's alloy ;
Thy radiant presence will the dark home brighten,
   In sorrow's drear abode spread light and joy.

War.

I HEAR the sound of desolating war,
    In fancy hear contending armies meet,
The clash of deadly weapons, and the roar
    Of flashing cannon, and the drum's loud beat :
As charge on charge of squadrons, fierce and fleet,
    Dash o'er the plain bedrenched with human gore,
Into the fiery battle's fiercest heat,
    Thence to return in glowing life no more,
    But at the will of kings their souls to Heaven restore.

And in the midst—where murderous batteries sweep
    With sanguinary aim—the mangled dead,
In grim, contorted shapes, lie heap on heap,
    The beauteous semblance of God's image fled.
And see the fatal shell burst overhead,
    Where crowded ranks advance in order deep,
To meet with gory wounds and slaughter red ;
    The stricken start, with wild, convulsive leap,—
    A moment's sudden pang, then sink to endless sleep.

What scenes of hellish strife ! what countless woes !
    A single tyrant's lust of conquest make !
Around his path the blood of nations flows,
    At his approach the thrones of empires shake,
And hearts of men with fear and trembling quake ;
    The rule of ancient kingdoms he o'erthrows,
His eager thirst of wealth and power to slake,
    Until his bloody days in darkness close,
    The 'frighted world but Death and Devastation knows.

And thou, Columbia,* that erst stood high
  Among the nations, great among the great,
Low in the dust thy vaunted honours lie,
  Gone is the wealth which did thy soul elate ;
No more canst thou of power supremest prate,
  And with imagin'd strength all earth defy,
For lo ! red Ruin hovers at thy gate,
  And dark Oppression with malignant eye,
  And greedy maw insatiate, lurks in ambush nigh.

In most ignoble strife thy sons are slain,
  With fratricidal war thy bosom torn ;
Thy countless dead encumber hill and plain,
  Thy pleasant land is naked and forlorn.
By tyrant law bereft thy widows mourn,
  And all the corners of the earth complain.
The world looks on with pity and with scorn,
  Where Hell's dark attributes alone doth reign,
  And Desolation stalks upon each fair domain.

In thy unholy strife thou seekest aid
  From Him whose Word doth Peace on Earth proclaim !
And when thine arms fresh butchery hath made,
  Thou dost blaspheme with thanks the Holy Name !
As though thy help from Sovereign Justice came,
  Whose sacred mandates thou hast disobeyed ;
Another Power thy gratitude may claim,
  To whom alone thou hast true homage paid,
  By deeds as dark as ever did fair Earth degrade.

* This poem was written when the American War was at its maddest height.

The world is full of strife, yea, life is war,
From youth to age a long and weary fight,
The struggling poor for bread, the rich to soar
Above his neighbour, to unrivall'd height.
Oh, that the world in friendship would unite,
All angry strife and jealous bickerings o'er,
And Peace encompass Earth with halo bright,
And radiant Progress march from shore to shore,
And War with all its evils cease for evermore.

Cash.

TO exist in the world, and escape all its woes,
To be favoured by friends, and be feared by foes,
To live cozy and careless, in fair days or foul,
With a stomach well stuff'd, and a satisfied soul,
You must cleverly catch all the cash that you can,
For it is by his money that man values man ;
Some would make us believe they consider it trash,
Yet every one likes to secure the " *Cash.*"

The rich rogue may strut in his "turkey-cock pride,"
For broad cloth he knows will his villany hide,
While the poor man must creep to his door for employ,
Whose merit is hidden beneath corduroy ;
The rich booby's flatter'd, and fuddled with praise,
While the poor genius rusts in neglect all his days ;
For character, talent, and all may "go smash,"
They are valueless each, if you haven't the " *Cash.*"

The " squire of broad acres," he reigns in his hall ;
How each lout on his lands for his least favours crawl !
And his tenantry tremble in dread of his ire,
For who is the man to be fear'd like the squire ?
What urchin so hardy his garden to break ?
What half-hunger'd wight may a fat rabbit take ?
He rides through the town in his carriage so flash,
And gets all the comforts of life with his " *Cash*."

The drainer works hard, and but little he earns,
To buy the bit duds for his wife and his bairns,
And crockery and coals and a thousand things more,—
As for victuals, but scanty and scarce is their store ;
Oft out of a job in the long winter's gloom,
Long bills lie unsettled, the meal-chest is toom ;
Yet he still struggles on, in despite of the " fash,"
Though his life is a burden for want of the " *Cash*."

'Tis said the first pair had to work for each meal,
They had pullets to " ploat," and potatoes to peel ;
And the curse would be carried their progeny through,
And that each man should live by the sweat of his brow ;
But many since then have a better dodge found,
Though they live on its fat, yet they till not the ground ;
They revel in luxury obtain'd without " fash,"
And their whole lives doth prove the importance of " *Cash*.'

The Soldier's Farewell.

FAREWELL to the home that hath shelter'd my childhood,
   Adieu to the land where my kindred abide ;
No more as a child shall I wander the wildwood,
   No more shall I visit the homes of Tyneside.

I have join'd the red army, my thoughts are of battle,
   Of danger and glory in countries afar,
Where the cavalry charge, and the loud cannon rattle,
   The pride, and the pomp, and the splendour of war.

Oh ! I hate this dull round of monotonous labour,
   A slave at the will of employers to live,
Whose study it is how to swindle his neighbour,
   So ready to grasp, so reluctant to give.

The lordling looks down with contempt on the lowly,
   And views with disdain the rough garments of toil ;
And the poor ape the rich in their vice and their folly.
   And bow at their feet, be they ever so vile.

But the soldier he lives in defiance of sorrow,
   Exempt from the cares that to other men cling ;
No trouble has he, nor thought of the morrow,
   Assur'd that each day its provision will bring.

And the gold for which men will their honesty barter,
   Doth seldom the hand of the soldier pollute ;
But with plentiful rations, his pipe, and his porter,
   And his kind girl beside him ; what better can suit ?

Then, farewell to my own native land ; I may never
  Return to the scenes of my childhood again,
But while I have breath I'll remember for ever
  My friends with affection, my foes with disdain.

Vale of Tyne.

VALE of Tyne ! sweet Spring returning
    Soon will deck thy groves again ;
When the lark awakes the morning
    With its sweet and soothing strain ;
When the trees their buds are showing,
And the bright spring-flowers are glowing
Where the zephyrs softly blowing,
    Scatter verdure on the plain.

Soon again shall beauteous Summer
    Clothe the fruitful fields with green,
Scattering pleasant odours from her,
    Strewing flowers to deck the scene ;
When the sunshine gilds the river,
Whose soft murmur ceases never,
Flowing down thy bosom ever,
    Those enamell'd banks between.

On the hill of Yarridge standing,
    In the summer twilight pale,
With enraptured gaze commanding
    All the beauties of the vale ;

Smiling fields are spread before us,
Blithesome larks are singing o'er us :
And the woodlands join in chorus,
   Sweet as songs of nightingale.

See the landscape far extending,
   Verdant lawns and meadows gay,
Till the ambient sky seems blending
   With the blue hills far away ;
See the quiet homesteads near ye,
Once I thought them dull and dreary,
Now of aimless wandering weary,
   Glad, contented I can stay.

The Northumbrian Exile.

MY old home stands among the hills,
   The far north hills, where blooms the heather,
Where early songs the laverick trills,
   Ere from the vale the white mists gather.

It overlooks a valley sweet,
   Through which doth wind a stately river ;
Green groves extend its brink to meet,
   And listen to its murmurs ever.

The azure hills afar are seen,
   Whose summits loom in frowning splendour ;
While pleasant valleys lie between,
   Where crystal streams in peace meander.

I oft would stray upon the hills,
  Amid the summer evening shadows,
Or down the vale, where trickling rills
  Sang lullaby among the meadows.

I love to roam at evening's close,
  And watch the golden stars appearing ;
All nature lies in hush'd repose,
  No jarring noise of life in hearing.

The music of the rolling spheres,
  And mellow sounds from distance coming ;
Soft harmony enchants my ears,
  Like fairies on their wee harps humming.

The Banks of Tyne are far away,
  Its woody slopes and ancient towers,
Its waving fields and meadows gay,
  Where erst I spent my youth's brief hours.

Shall e'er I look on Tynedale more,
  Or view the hills of Hexhamshire ?
I often stand upon the shore,
  And homeward gaze with fond desire.

Though here the sun sheds endless light,
  Where palm trees wave by flashing fountains ;
I long to see the heather bright,
  That crowns Northumbria's misty mountains,

I never see a friend's dear face,
  Nor hear love's soothing accents spoken ;
Self, self alone, doth rule our race,
  Which all their daily acts betoken.

Would I were on the hills once more,
   When winter's storms are fiercely driving ;
To hear the sullen tempests roar,
   Like angry fiends in fury striving.

Why did I leave my native home,
   And from the friends of childhood sever ?
May I return, no more to roam,
   But live in peace, in peace for ever.

England.

LET Freedom reign in England,
   Let Freedom ever reign ;
For the stalwart sons of the sea-girt isle
   Will never wear the chain.
The cheering star of liberty
   Shines over all the land ;
A heritage our fathers won,
   By strong determin'd hand.

Let Justice reign in England,
   Let equal justice reign ;
And they who fill her seat may still
   Her glorious rights maintain.
For the people have a voice—
   A voice that will be heard—
A voice which hath a mighty sway,
   When by Oppression stirr'd.

Let Valour reign in England,
　　To guard our pleasant land,
To drive the rash invader back,
　　Who dares pollute the strand,
There are a thousand victories
　　Recorded to her name ;
And Englishmen will still uphold
　　Their brave forefathers' fame.

Let unity in England,
　　Its strength and safeguard live :
Then to the foes who threat our shores,
　　We may defiance give.
Then wealth shall flow on England,
　　As rivers to the sea :
And Peace shall smile throughout the isle,
　　Where dwell the brave and free.

Death's Dominion.

MILLIONS are gone to his dark domain,
　　By many a dreary path ;
A countless throng, they onward strain,
To swell the ranks of that dismal train,
　　In the vast empire of Death.

There they are met from every clime—
  From countries everywhere :
The mighty men of the olden time,
Renown'd for cruelty and crime,
  Are all assembled there.

The countless host of warriors brave
  In a thousand battles slain ;
The haughty king and the crouching slave,
They all are equal in the grave,
  Where Death supreme doth reign.
Tyrants who held the world in dread
  Now lie dissolv'd in clay ;
The humble labourer may tread
Above the haughty lordling's head,
  Who spurn'd him yesterday.

The eager youth of noble aim,
  Inspired with genius rare,
Who cherish'd hopes of deathless fame,
Until the fell Destroyer came,
  And quench'd them in despair.
The old man whose long life had pass'd,
  For self alone employed ;
And when the summons came at last,
Regretful looks were backward cast
  At precious time destroy'd.

Day after day fresh thousands go
  To swell the motley crowd ;
The same dread fate we all must know,
The gay and gloomy, high and low,
  The slavish and the proud :

We all are hastening to our doom,
    In the same dismal path ;
To change the fair earth's beauteous bloom
For the damp air of the sullen tomb,
    The dark abode of Death.

" Dear Love, the Spring has come again."

DEAR love, the spring has come again—
    The flowery spring, the joyous spring ;
The sunshine glows on hill and plain,
    And gladdens every living thing.

Now is the season of delight,
    The dark and gloomy days are o'er ;
Then let me seek thy presence bright,
    And meet thy kind embrace once more.

And let thy breath's delicious balm,
    Like woodland perfumes, fan my cheek ;
And let thy voice with music calm,
    In angel's sweetest accents speak.

Thy voice is like the soothing lay
    That syrens of the ocean sing ;
Thy breath is like the breath of May,
    With odours sweet from genial spring.

Thy glance is like the morning beam
    That doth the orient hills illume ;
Thy face is sweet as poet's dream,
    Where white and red fresh roses bloom.

And on that matchless form of thine
    Are Nature's fairest gifts bestowed ;
The queenly brow is Virtue's shrine,
    Thy pure heart is Love's abode.

I bow beneath thy beauty's sway,
    An eager, earnest devotee ;
My life before thy feet I lay,
    Which would be joyless wanting thee.

But should my pleadings fail to sway
    Love's sweet emotion in thy breast ;
Still thou in paths Elysian stray,
    While I exist by love unblest.

May never dark misfortune lour,
    Nor this harsh world thy acts condemn ;
But life be peaceful as the flower
    That swings upon its trembling stem.

Live happy, whilst my heart contains
    A world of griefs with comfort none ;
Pleasure for thee on earth remains,
    For me is rest in heaven alone.

And go where happy amours live,
    In smiling fields of pleasure rove ;
If others false ovations give,
    I offer thee a deathless love.

Retrospections.

THE bright glow from the mountain is driven,
  The last gleam from the river is gone ;
And the stars deck the deep vault of heaven,
  While I sit, to my thoughts all alone.
On the deeds of the past will I ponder—
  On the friends and the loves known before ;
And in fancy again let me wander
  Through the scenes to be view'd nevermore.

Oh, I mourn for the pleasures now over,
  And I grieve that the past is no more ;
For my weary heart ne'er will recover
  That repose which did charm it before.
The false pomp of the hollow world scorning,
  From the cares of the mad world away,
I arose with the lark in the morning
  To the toil of the long summer day.

In the stillness of eventide roaming,
  By the side of the sweet river Tyne,
When the world lay at peace in the gloaming,
  What dreams of the future were mine !
But how empty the dreams that were cherish'd,
  They have faded in gloom and despair !
And the hopes of my boyhood have perish'd,
  Bequeathing but sorrow and care.

Smiling Hope, how thy promises flatter !
  What radiant illusions we see !
Till the world's stern realities scatter
  The visions created by thee.
For this life is a hard struggle ever—
  A wearisome journey and long—
Where each man with his might must endeavour,
  And the weak are a prey to the strong.

Oh Happiness ! long have I sought thee,
  But thou hidest thy heaven-lit face,
Still eluding my grasp when I thought thee
  Secure in my eager embrace.
In the bower where Beauty is present,
  And Love doth illumine the scene,
Thou art there with a smile evanescent,
  Till the shadows of grief come between.

Man's follies and passions make dreary
  The brightness and beauty of earth ;
And the sorrowful wail of the weary
  May be heard 'mid the revellers' mirth.
But afar through the sky's glowing portals
  There is rest on that bright summer shore ;
And the songs of the ransom'd immortals
  In its mansions are heard evermore.

The Military Execution.

THE noise of merriment is hush'd,
  The revellers all are fled ;
Where late the mirthful music gush'd,
  Is silent as the dead.

Confined within his narrow cell,
  The soldier waits his doom ;
He hears the solemn midnight bell
  Toll out amid the gloom.

" Another day has come," he cries,
  " The last that I shall see ;
No more the sun will climb the skies,
  To light the world for me,

" For I must die, by man condemn'd.
  A victim to the laws,—
The cruel laws by tyrants fram'd.
  To suit their wicked cause.

" But scorn unmeasured shall be hurl'd
  At them with latest breath ;
I'll laugh defiance to the world,
  And glad shake hands with death.

" For care hath cast its gloomy shroud
  Around life's dreary way ;
The harsh behests of tyrants proud,
  I daily must obey.

" But, oh ! I've home and kindred ties—
    A wife and children three ;
I know they wait with eager eyes,
    And open arms for me.

" But never more my constant feet
    Shall home delighted stray ;
The kind and welcome smile to greet
    Of lov'd ones far away.

" My comrades, we have fac'd the storm,
    And stood the battle-strife ;
Your hands reluctant will perform
    The deed that takes my life.

" The earth will smile as heretofore
    Beneath the summer ray ;
The birds will carol as of yore
    Through many a glowing day.

" Arise, my soul ! man's wrath defy,
    Thou wilt be past it soon ;
With head erect, and dauntless eye,
    I'll face the firm platoon."
    *   *   *   *

The sunbeams slant along the plain,
    And wake the camp to life,
And light ungrateful man again
    To deeds of blood and strife.

Beyond the lines behold him stand,
    A bearing proud he wears,
And faces firm the little band
    Of stalwart musketeers.

Their arms are raised with deadly aim,
    Each fatal bullet flies ;
And for a fault that bears no blame,
    Their gallant comrade dies.

Mons Calpe.*

MONS Calpe stands where the oceans meet
    By Andalusia's shore ;
And the restless waves around its feet
    Make music evermore.
I've stood on Calpe's frowning steep,
    When wild the wind did blow,
And watch'd the kingly eagle sweep
    A thousand feet below.

I've stood on Calpe's summit high,
    And watch'd the sunset bright,
When a thousand ships were sailing by,
    Away to the silent night.
The light zephyrs kiss'd the sea,
    And filled the snow-white sails,
And stole the breath of the orange tree
    From many balmy vales.

* "MONS CALPE," the ancient name of Gibraltar. The Author resided three
years and a half at Gibraltar, when serving in the Corps of Royal Engineers.

From great Mons Calpe's rugged side
　　The dark artillery frown ;
From embrasure and loop-hole wide
　　They look defiance down.
Old England's flag triumphant waves
　　Above its lofty head ;
And England's sons in countless graves,
　　In its defence have bled.

From Calpe's cloudy top surveyed,
　　High hills extend afar,
And fertile vales where erst was played
　　The glorious game of war.
The deep sea laves the rocky strand,
　　Oft strewn with heaps of slain,
When gallant Elliott's little band
　　Withstood the hosts of Spain.

Oh ! happy were we on Calpe's hill,
　　Blithe comrades all and free ;
The frantic world kept hurrying still,
　　But never a care had we.
The Calpean girls have raven curls,
　　And eyes that beam divine ;
We wooed the girls with the raven curls,
　　And drank the Xeres wine.

My soul Love's sweet control obeyed,
　　'Mid Nature's wonders grand,
Till I bade farewell to the Calpean maid,
　　And left that summer land.

And again I sought my native clime,
  From comrades loth to part ;
But the memories of that happy time
  Shall live within my heart.

The Conscience-Stricken.

THERE is a weight upon his heart—
  A weary weight which ever presses,
A grief that never will depart,
  But day and night his soul possesses.

He mingles in the giddy crowd,
  Their evanescent mirth to borrow ;
He eager joins the revel loud,
  And tries to laugh away his sorrow.

He eager drains the maddening glass,
  By drowning care, destroying reason :
Resolving, as the moments pass,
  To wait that " more convenient season."

But when the swinish feast is o'er,
  And thought comes back with sober morning—
With self-brought misery in store,
  And care a hundred-fold returning.

Ah ! then the follies and the sins
    By him committed loom before him ;
And dark despondency begins
    To cast its baleful shadow o'er him.

The summer beauties of the earth—
    The day-star's glory fails to cheer him ;
Dark suicidal thoughts have birth,
    Dark spirits lurk in ambush near him.

Remorseful feelings rack his breast,
    Their wild commotion still increases ;
The troubled conscience will not rest,
    Its gnawing anguish never ceases.

The scorn of men he must abide,
    No sympathetic voice to waken ;
Condemn'd in misery to hide,
    A weary waif, by all forsaken.

The World's Opinion.

GO, Conscience, monitor of man,
    At duty's high behest ;
Let each his daily conduct scan
    With thy unfailing test ;
For every one delights to see
What may his neighbour's failings be,
    Yet blind with self-esteem,

To probe his own he will not try ;
Therefore, the world's opinions I
    Of little value deem.

The Pharisee may thunder down
    Our condemnation sure ;
The pompous magistrate may frown
    Upon the fallen poor ;
Professors proud, self-satisfied,
May " pass by on the other side,"
    As though they knew not sin.
The sanctimonious crowds that go
To Sabbath fanes for outward show,
    Yet blind and dark within.

The upstart, who but yesterday
    To earn a crust was fain,
Will now his apish acts display,
    That honest men disdain ;
And labour, each man's heritage,
His greatest need from age to age,
    E'en cringing lacqueys scorn ;
Labour, that should more honour'd be
Than all the pomp and pageantry
    Of fools to titles born.

If thou dost man's vain plaudits prize,
    Earth's glittering treasures win ;
For toil's rough garb all ranks despise,
    And poverty is sin ;
But trust not for a single hour

The slave who crawls to pride and power,
        And courts the rich man's smile ;
And him disdain who lives for self,
Whose sole aim is to gather pelf,
        By every sneaking wile.

Staward-le-Peel.

Written on the occasion of the Annual Pic-nic of the Langley Temperance
Society.

ON the banks of the Allen in sweet summer time,
    When nature exults in her beautiful prime ;
When the bees are abroad, and the birds are in tune,
And the happy lark sings to the flower-deckt June ;
When the gleam of the river doth gladden the eye,
With the green of the earth and the glow of the sky ;—
Then a rapture divine the poet doth feel,
Surveying the beauties of Staward-le-Peel.

Oh ! the many-hued meadows their perfumes bestow,
Where the musical Allen is murmuring low ;
And the woodlands extend in their garments of green,
That are clasp'd by the sun in its glorious sheen ;
Its golden beams darting their foliage through,
Begild with their brightness each leaf laden bough ;
And the light-winged zephyrs doth playfully steal
Round the picturesque ruins of Staward-le-Peel.

Go, visit fair Staward, and stand on its height,
Its glories survey with a rapturous delight ;

Look down in the depths of the gorge far below,
Where the confluent streams on their rocky beds flow :
And view the steep slope of the craggy ravine,
Where the tall trees extend their umbrageous green ;
And the quick darting falcon majestic doth wheel
Round the cliffs frowning grandly at Staward-le-Peel.

But Saturday witness'd a gathering rare
Of mirth-loving swains and of nymphs debonair ;
All the beauty of Allendale thitherward hied,
With the fairest and choicest from bonny Tyneside.
Like flowers that glow in some Eastern land,
Bewildering the sense with variety grand ;
So these exquisite beauties their charms did reveal,
Our hearts to bring captive from Staward-le-Peel.

The music rings sweet through each dingle and nook ;
But to far other sounds once their echoes awoke,
When murder was rife in the rude days of old,
And this was the stronghold of freebooters bold.
Now the shopman and clerk they may dance on the sod,
Where the red-handed chief and the warrior trod ;
And teetotal speakers their tenets reveal,
Where the wassailers revell'd at Staward-le-Peel.

But slowly the shadows creep over the scene,
And the bevy of beauties disperse from the green
With their true-loving swains over daisy-deckt leas,
Through bye-paths secluded and shaded by trees ;
And soft words are spoken, and loving vows paid,
Sweet promises given by each happy maid ;
Till the shade-mantled night for awhile doth conceal
The grandeur and glory of Staward-le-Peel.

"Come, love, with me."

COME, love, with me, where summer blooms,
  And beauty decks the earth ;
And air redolent with perfumes
  Invites the soul to mirth ;
And sunshine gloriously illumes
  Each flower at its birth.

Come where the leafy branches meet,
  From noontide's ardent glare ;
Come where the rose-embowered seat
  Emits a fragrance rare ;
The lark will sing in strains more sweet,
  Dear love, when thou art there.

The flower-bespangled paths look gay,
  Where golden sunlight gleams ;
The bee and butterfly all day
  Disport beneath its beams ;
We'll pass the balmy hours away
  In love's Elysian dreams.

How can my burning love be told ?
  What mind its depths can trace ?
Thy yielding form I will enfold
  In loving, long embrace ;
Content thy beauty to behold,
  Adorn'd with angel grace.

The bright world waits with ready smile,
  Thy glowing youth to greet ;
Thy young heart never felt its guile,
  Or witness'd its deceit.
Then from each dark, ensnaring wile,
  Good angels guard thy feet.

Come, love, with me, where glad larks soar
  Beyond the leafy grove ;
Thy presence will my heart restore,
  When anxious troubles move ;
I feel as though I lived once more
  In boyhood's dream of love.

"When the Ship comes in."

MY ship went out on the summer sea,
  On a bright and breezy day,
When like a sheet on the summer sea,
  The glittering sunshine lay.
The verdant hills that fringed the shore,
  Were wrapt in glorious sheen,
Where the happy birds sang evermore
  In bowers of emerald green.

Away, away, my buoyant bark,
  Across the flashing spray ;
I watched her sails till the evening dark,
  As she bravely bore away.

Away, away, like a living thing
　　Upon the breathing sea,—
Like a living thing sent forth to bring
　　Bright treasures back to me.

The changeful years have passed away
　　With sorrow in their train,
But the ship that sailed that shining day
　　Returns not back again.
I've watched from dawn till twilight pale,
　　Through all these weary days,
Yet never could see her snow-white sail
　　'Mid ocean's purple haze.

Embayed where endless summer smiles,
　　She waits the welcome breeze;
Or saileth among the balmy isles
　　Of the sunny southern seas.
My ship is laden with choicest things
　　From many a far-off land ;
The wealth of India's courts she brings,
　　With pearls from Persia's strand,

All wasting fears behind I'll cast,
　　And loose the reins to mirth,
When the welcome ship comes in at last
　　With the rarest gifts of earth ;—
Choice gifts the sentient soul to please,
　　Unmix'd with grief's alloy,
To make the world a bower of ease,
　　A Paradise of joy.

" Oh ! when will the ship come in again ?"
Is the weary mourner's wail ;
And sad eyes gaze on the cheerless main
To view its welcome sail.
But they toil, toil on through a struggling life—
The world's unceasing din ;
Yet hoping ever the storm and strife
Will end when the ship comes in.

At Elsdon.

HAE ye ivver been at Elsdon ?—
The world's unfinish'd neuk ;
It stands amaug the hungry hills,
An' wears a frozen leuk.
The Elsdon folks like dicin' stegs
At ivvery stranger stare ;
An' hather broth an' curlew eggs
Ye'll get for supper there.

Yeu neet aw cam tiv Elsdon
Sair tired efter dark ;
Aw'd travell'd mony a leynsome meyle
Wet through the varra sark.
Maw legs were warkin' fit ta brik,
An' empty was me kite,
But nowther love nor money could
Get owther bed or bite.

At ivvery hoose iv Elsdon
    Aw teld me desperate need,
But nivver a corner had the churls
    Where aw might lay me heed ;
Sae at the public-hoose aw boos'd
    Till aw was sent away ;
Then tiv a steyble-loft aw crept,
    Au' coil'd amang the hay.

Should the Frenchers land iv England,
    Just gie them Elsdon fare ;
By George ! they'll sharply hook it back,
    Au' nivver cum ne mair.
For a hungry hole like Elsdon,
    Aw nivver yit did see ;
An' if aw gan back tiv Elsdon,
    " The de'il may carry me."

The Flower of the Flock.

THE flower of all the flock is gone
    Through heaven's shining portals ;
She stands before the great white throne,
    Among the bright immortals.

Her life was like the sun-flower bright
    In summer's evanescence ;
But now her home hath lost the light
    Of her angelic presence.

THE FLOWER OF THE FLOCK.

With hope-delighted eyes they saw
　Their bud of promise flourish ;
So tender flowers in sunshine glow,
　But with the cold winds perish.

She gaily tripp'd life's thorny road,
　A loving, joyous creature ;
The pure light of heaven glow'd
　On every happy feature.

Her voice was music soft and calm,
　That charmed each new comer :
Her presence shed a soothing balm,—
　The sweetest flower of summer.

She sleeps now in the graveyard lone
　With dear ones gone before her ;
The winter wind in mournful tone
　Of sadness sigheth o'er her.

Shed not for her the bitter tears,
　Nor grieve with vain repining ;
The palm of victory she bears,
　In highest heaven shining.

From this harsh world its many woes
　He did her soul deliver ;
She lives in fellowship with those
　Who hymn His praises ever.

The March of Progress.

Written for the " Hexham Courant" on the occasion of the first anniversary
of that newspaper.

GOD said, " Let there be light," and light sprang forth
   In bright effulgence from His crystal throne :
Its boundless ray illumed the embryo earth,
   And through unmeasured space resplendent shone.

A crude and shapeless void, the vast orb lay,
   Till form was given by His mighty hand ;
And earth was deck'd in beautiful array,
   And myriad creatures peopled sea and land.

This wondrous world and all it doth contain,
   Was made for man in long delight to dwell ;
But Sin appeared with darkness in its train,
   And all the noisome evils nurs'd in hell.

Grim War, with flaming visage, came ere long,
   And man in every cruel art grew skill'd ;
The weak were driven to obey the strong,
   The strong with pride and lust of power were fill'd.

Long ages, with their deeds have pass'd away,
   Nor saved a record from oblivion's tomb ;
And mighty kingdoms lived their little day,
   That rose in darkness and resank in gloom.

O'er countless tribes the sable cloud was cast ;
  They groped in darkness to the silent grave ;
Each unto Death for aye forgotten past,—
  The pampered tyrant and the panting slave.

Again the Almighty said " Let there be light ;"
  Lo ! in the east appeared a brighter dawn ;
And Gospel truths dispell'd the darksome night,
  And Christian tenets were reveal'd to man.

O'er many nations spread the kindling ray ;
  On lands remote the germs of Truth were cast ;
Though weeds of Error come with rank decay,
  Yet Truth shall flourish full, mature at last.

Though venal teachers may false doctrines spread,
  And jealous creeds a constant warfare wage ;
Though feeble souls in blind belief are led,
  And shallow bigots fume with helpless rage.

Yet shall the light of Progress, brighter grown,
  The mists of doubt and ignorance dispel ;
And strife and deadly hate be things unknown,
  But all mankind in peace and concord dwell.

There is a power that wields a potent sway,
  It worketh silent but with sure success,
It keepeth Wrong and Tyranny at bay,
  And Right and Truth are strengthen'd by THE PRESS.

The meanest hind who tills the stubborn soil,
  Of knowledge may the richest treasures choose ;
Though poor, depress'd, and bound to daily toil,
  The page of wisdom he may glad peruse.

For labour is the heritage of all—
    The world's necessity—our chiefest need—
The curse pronounc'd on Adam at his fall,
    And to his race eternally decreed.

Then ne'er repine at thy unhappy lot,
    Though Wealth may flaunt its splendour to thy gaze ;
Heaven's high mandate he obeyeth not,
    Who doth in ease inglorious spend his days.

Labour, thy true nobility assert,
    Keep onward in the path of Progress still;
Let Nature's beauties cheer thy drooping heart,
    Its glorious teachings to thy mind instil.

Behold the green, enamell'd summer hills,
    The gorgeous beauty of the vales survey,
Where the sweet lark its song melodious trills,
    The long bright hours of the summer day.

Or when the day its dying glory flings
    Through all the glowing west in golden floods,
When gentle zephyrs move on perfum'd wings,
    And whisper " hush" unto the listening woods.

Or when the night begins her tranquil reign,
    And far-off worlds appear in boundless space.—
Vast worlds wide-scattered through the empyreal main,
    That round their regal suns great circles trace.

Then contemplate the nothingness of man,
    What strange conceit from dust and ashes came;
The apish airs that pride of pelf puts on,
    Might bring from angels' eyes the tears of shame.

" Let there be light," our doubting minds to clear;
  Our grovelling souls to higher aims will soar;
Rejoice, O Earth ! behold the dawn appear,
  When Truth will shine in beauty evermore.

The Harvest Time.

THE hues of harvest now adorn
    The fields which smile before the farmer;
The breezes wave the ripening corn,
    And through the greenwood gently murmur.

The rustle of the golden grain
    Sounds like an old and pleasant story;
When sunshine rests upon the plain,
    And covers all the hills with glory.

Though now within the dells are mute
    The merry song-birds' tuneful voices,
The gardens teem with flowers and fruit,
    And Earth with plenteous yield rejoices.

And all adown Tyne's bonny vale
    The bounteous load they're homeward bringing ;
The fragrant field and fruitful dale,
    Are with sweet harvest music ringing.

Away upon the heathy fells
    We'll wander in the quiet gloaming ;
For there among the heather bells,
    The honey bee all day is roaming.

We'll rest beside the waters clear
    That trickle past the leafy bowers ;—
The hum of myriad insects near—
    The music of the noonday hours.

Oh, there are memories sublime
    Of happy days amid the wildwood,—
Sweet memories of the harvest time,
    That gild the brightest scenes of childhood.

But now those happy days are gone,
    Returning with their freshness never ;
This weary heart is sere and lone,
    And dead to all enjoyment ever.

"I bade my Lyre a last Farewell."

I BADE my lyre a last farewell,
    Resolv'd the world no more should hear
Its sober strains, which as they fell,
    Did but evoke the spiteful sneer ;
For fools usurp the critics' right,
And worthless deem what I indite.

Yet haply there are honest hearts
 That vibrate to its quiet tone,
To whom its music joy imparts ;
 I strike my lyre for these alone,
Not for the soul wrapt up in self,
Who values everything by pelf.

Great minds have proved their marvellous might,
 Whose names on history's page will shine,
Who brought immortal truths to light,
 And cast the glittering pearls to swine ;
The grovelling herd the prize obtain'd,
No meed their benefactors gain'd.

Awake, my lyre, to higher themes
 Than e'er thou hast essayed before ;
My soul shall bask in beauty's beams,
 The golden realms of truth explore.
And by untrodden paths pursue
All that is beautiful and true.

Let wisdom's ray illume the mind,
 Life's dark deformities to bare,
The faults and follies of mankind,
 The hollow world's delusive glare,
The shams and vanities which are
With truth and honesty at war.

My lyre, thy quiet music fills
 My heart with feelings light and gay,
As sunshine on the summer hills,
 Or happy schoolboy's holiday.
Let slaves to Mammon's altar throng,
But let me wield the power of song.

Hexham Abbey.

O, MERRILY ring the Hexham bells
   The Tynedale woods among ;
Re-echoing through the tuneful dells,
Dying away on the distant fells,
    Where the lavrock trills its song.
The Abbey rears its lofty head
    Above the massive pile ;
A thousand changeful years have fled
Since first the stately monks did tread
    Each grandly-cloister'd aisle.

That ancient fane could tell a tale
    Of doings dark and dread ;
When Scottish raiders scoured the vale,
Leaving a charred and bloody trail,
    By greedy rapine led.
Then would the dread war-beacon fling
    Its glare from hill to hill ;
Then would the Tyne-men's war-shout ring,
Each warrior to his weapon spring,
    With deadly, desperate will.

But now a grand and gorgeous scene
    The pensive stranger views ;
Rich fields extend in their garb of green,
And the ancient forests stretch between,
    In many gorgeous hues.

And sumptuous wealth has dwellings grand
    Amid the woodlands green ;
And the humble homes of Labour stand
All over the face of the smiling land,
    Where his handiwork is seen.

For Labour is lord of the teem'ng earth,
    And he wears a kingly mien ;
His stalwart sons in their strength went forth,
And the wilderness woke to joy and mirth,
    Wherever their hands had been.
Great cities sprang on the silent shore,
    And over the isles forlorn ;
And a happier smile the summer wore,
To see the desolate waste no more,
    But fields of golden corn.

O, sweetly chime the Hexham bells,
    On the quiet Sabbath day ;
And a pleasing tale their music tells,
Re-echoing through the peaceful dells,
    As the people meet to pray.
Long may the stately Abbey stand
    To grace our pleasant town ;
And let the light of truth expand,
And progress shine o'er all the land,
    Where Tyne meanders down.

Midnight Musings.

MUSING on bygone days in the silent watch of night,
  When the moon has wrapped the vale in its soft and
  dreamy light ;
And the stars look calmly down on the quiet world below,
Where the stately rivers murmur as ocean-ward they flow.

There is no sound of life, nor sigh, nor whisper heard,
Save what the dark pines give by the solemn night-wind
  stirr'd ;
And the peace, pervading earth, my weary heart hath found,
For my soul partakes the calm which filleth all around.

The moon looks from above with a tranquil beaming eye,
Throwing rays along the path where the withered leaves do
  lie ;
Filling the open fields with a flood of mellow light ;
With its soft and silvery radiance giving beauty to the night.

Now gazing down the vista of the long departed years,
What a scene of light and shadow before mine eyes appears !
I see the flowery paths where my careless boyhood strayed,
And the marks of many struggles in life's rough journey made.

I see the genial faces of the lov'd of long ago,
The friends whose kindly solace it was bliss indeed to know;
And I see the idiot sneer which the slave in power wore,
Whose words of empty scorn with writhing pain I bore.

Life is a fitful season, with its fair days and its foul,
Then never to blank despair like a craven yield thy soul ;
To-day, no refuge nigh, the ruthless storm may beat,
The sunny morrow comes, and thy fancied woes retreat.

'Tis man who makes the strife that mars the beauteous earth,
Himself creates the sorrows attendant from his birth ;
Let the reign of Peace begin, the ray of Progress shine,
And the happy world will smile in the light of truth divine.

Then man shall greet his neighbour in fellowship and love,
Good-will to all mankind be heralded above ;
And kindness dwell on earth as the sheen upon the river ;
And the star of peace will burn for ever and for ever.

New Year Thoughts.

THE chill breath of winter creeps over the leas—
    Down the dells where the dead leaves are lying :
And it seemeth to sing through the skeleton trees,
    A dirge to the year that is dying.

The old year will pass to eternity's void,
    The pleasures it brought us are over;
The bright glowing hours whose calm we enjoyed,
    Where memory delighted will hover.

Oh, happy the man whose retrospect wears
   The glory his good deeds have given :
His mind is untroubled by earth's common cares,
   For his hope and his trust are in heaven.

The years with new honours pass over his head,
   The great and the gifted revere him,
And the motes of mankind by his influence led,
   From their giddy pursuits hover near him.

Lo ! the year has its birth 'mid the cold winter's gloom,
   When nature all chilly reposes ;
But the spring will return with its verdure and bloom,
   And the summer will come with its roses.

So our path may seem rugged in life's early stage,
   And fortune be slow with her favour,
Yet hope is the star that will guide us to age,
   And will strengthen each earnest endeavour.

And now is the season when love should expand,
   And words of kind comfort be spoken ;
Let Peace have its dwelling all over the land,
   And its reign be for ever unbroken.

To each and to all then " a happy new year ;"
   Cease malice so dark and distressing ;
And give to the poor, he will relish thy cheer,
   And give to thy neighbour a blessing.

Sonnet.

LO, beauty doth our admiration claim,
  To age and wisdom reverence due we give ;
To bards and heroes old of deathless fame,
  Whose mighty names will Time itself outlive.
But humble Virtue merits more esteem,
  More truthful homage than to these belong ;
Her quiet charms supply a higher theme
  For man's example, and for poet's song.
Lovely is virtue, and of untold worth,—
  In lowly cottage beautiful to see,—
A brighter ornament to noble birth
  Than all the grandeur won from high degree.
Virtue in woman claims our utmost love,
Exalted far all grosser thoughts above.

Nebuchadnezzar's Doom.

THE king looked forth from his palace,
　　Where mighty Babylon lies,
Whose stately towers and gorgeous fanes,
　　Sun-gilded, meet the skies.
The people thronged the glittering streets,
　　That rose in order grand ;
And the noise of music and merriment
　　Was heard through all the land.
The wealth of many a golden clime
　　Came crowding east and west ;
And hosts of ready warriors wait
　　To do the King's behest.

And pride inflamed the heart of the King,
　　As he looked in grandeur forth ;
And he spake high words that ill became
　　A creature form'd of earth :—
" Have I not built proud Babylon
　　In strength and splendour bright,
Where I the lord of earth may dwell
　　In majesty and might ;
The merchandise of every land
　　Comes thronging to its mart ;
Have I not all the wide earth yields
　　To satisfy my heart ?"

But while he spake a voice from heaven
    Hath staid his idle boast ;—
"O King, thy regal power hath fled,
    Thy kingdom thou hast lost,
And they shall drive thee forth from men,
    With beasts that range the fields ;
Thy sumptuous fare shall be exchanged
    For what the desert yields.
Till thou dost own a mightier Lord,
    Thy seven years' doom fulfil,—
That God most High doth kingdoms rule,
    And gives to whom He will."

Then shadows fell upon his mind,
    And reason left his soul ;
The King who but an hour before,
    Did all the world control.
And, driven forth from men's abodes,
    With lowing kine he fled ;
Till seven long years with sun and storm,
    Had passed above his head.
His nails like claws of birds became ;
    His hair like feathers grew ;
His body was scorch'd by the noonday's heat,
    And wet with the night's chill dew.

His doom was ended, and the light
    Illumed his soul at length ;
And Babylon's monarch stood again
    In kingly power and strength.
But homage meek was paid to Him,
    By whom his breath was given.

Who works His will o'er all the earth,
   And rules the hosts of heaven ;
Who doth the daring hearts of men
   To low abasement bring ;
And the meanest beggar in all his realms
   Is peer to the proudest king.

"How d'ye like the Rock ?"

THE Calpean Rock's a wondrous place ;
   Its rugged top seems touching heaven ;
With batteries all along its base,
   And galleries through its bowels driven.

Its works are terrible to view,
   And will for ages long endure ;
Big guns at every point peer through,
   From loop-hole black, and embrazure.

Old Gib is where the monkeys dine,
   With gust, on prickly pears and lemon ;
The easy natives drink sour wine,
   And make sad love to sulky women.

The girls may never stir abroad.
   But when their old duenna wishes ;
And oil and garlic is their food,
   With maccaroni, snails, and fishes.

The soldiers have their share of work—
Of plaguey drill and duty here, too,—
Plenty of punishment and pork,
Morocco beef, and mawkish beer, too.

But on this savage looking spot
There's no amusement nice and handy ;
And no diversion can be got,
Except you crack your brain with brandy.

Like felon prisoners we are set
Upon this Rock of limestone naked ;
Across the " Lines" we cannot get,
But here must stick till thorough baked.

They ask us how we like the Rock ;—
Too closely circumscribed its limit ;
Its length a short half-hour's walk,
Its height—I would not like to climb it.

We see the hills and vales of Spain,
The shady groves and winding river ;
I'd like the Rock as well again,
If I had seen it never.

NOTE.—The foregoing satire was written at Gibraltar. At that time there were few places in the garrison where the soldiers could profitably spend their time when off duty. The consequence was an excess of drunkenness and crime. However, before I left, an enterprising and philanthropic officer (Lieut. Jackson, R.A.) had splendid and capacious reading rooms opened, with a gymnasium adjoining ; refreshment and billiard rooms, &c. The officers gave lectures and readings in the evenings. This project did a vast amount of good. Similar institutions have since been erected in the principal garrisons at home and abroad.
I have mentioned snails as being an article of food used by the natives of Gibraltar. It is fact ; and very palatable food too, when cooked after their method.
When I went to Gibraltar soldiers were not permitted to enter the Spanish territory. Leave, however, was granted, with certain restrictions, before I came away.
" How d'ye like the Rock" is generally the first salutation new arrivals receive at Gibraltar.

The Struggles of Genius.

O YE, who dwell in sumptuous halls,
    And feel but self-created cares,—
Even excess of pleasure palls,
    And fancy oft vague sorrow shares,—
Your daily bread is ever sure,
    The morrow's comforts are prepar'd,—
Yea, luxuries, whereof the poor
    Have never mention heard.

There are among wealth's pamper'd crew,
    Those souless things whose only aim
Is but to seek enjoyment new,
    And fuel fresh to feed the flame.
The slaves who pander to their taste,
    And fawn beneath their proud disdain ;
These batten on the gold they waste
    In pleasures weak and vain.

The poor man in his lowly cot,
    Upon whose strength the rich depends,
Has for reward the wretched lot
    Of one whose labour never ends ;
For when his arm, erst strong and brave,
    No more can furnish daily want,
The parish dole, the pauper's grave,
    Are all his fellows grant.

But yet amid the ranks of toil,
   Though Fate her hostile weapons hurl'd,
Great minds have burst the heavy coil,
   And proved their strength before the world.
Of such was Burns, whose glorious name
   Will ne'er 'mid storms of Time be lost,
Who could not pelf, nor portion claim,
   Yet Scotia's proudest boast.

The chequer'd years still onward roll,
   And still his matchless songs are heard;
And men admire the regal soul
   Of Ayrshire's ploughman, Scotland's bard.
Life's dreariest ways the poet trod;
   The world, which gave but toil and strife,
Now worships as a demi-god,
   The genius wrong'd in life.

Those gaudy motes mis-named the great,
   Who wear the titles men bestow;
Death makes them doff their rank and state,
   They leave no name nor trace below.
Yet Burns, whose daily dole of bread
   His daily labour did supply,
Though gone among the countless dead
   His name will never die.

Go, mark the utterances sublime
   Of Chatterton, the wond'rous boy,
Whom, ere his genius reach'd its prime,
   The world's indifference did destroy;

He perish'd by its cold neglect,
   He bore the pangs of wounded pride,
He saw that all his hopes were wreck'd,
   And fell—a suicide.

Oh, many a soaring spirit lives
   In mean abodes, unknown, obscure;
And genius oft unsparing gives
   Her inspiration to the poor.
The world's support they seldom find,
   And prejudice their works deride;
They yet leave burning truths behind,
   Men's doubtful steps to guide.

The Old Love.

COME, cheer my heart with a song,
   For 'tis filled with grief to-day ;
Alas ! the love that I cherish'd so long,
   I cannot drive away.

Two eyes look up to mine
   With a sweet confiding gaze,—
Two pleading eyes where love doth shine
   In sad, soul-melting rays.

Up through the vale of years
  A voice of music calls,
And a form of angel light appears
  In memory's golden halls.

The tranquil day is o'er,
  And fall the twilight shades ;
But we shall wander again no more
  Among the forest glades.

On a quiet eve like this
  We swore affection true ;
Yet I madly spurn'd the offered bliss
  That rose to my eager view.

The seasons onward roll
  In their ever-changing course ;
While the venom of grief corrodes my soul,
  Weighed down by chill remorse.

The Old Pastor.

AROUND the little village church
  Were pleasant footpaths made ;
The green boughs waved above its porch.
  Where gorgeous sun-tints played.

And there was heard the sound of prayer
  Amid the Sabbath calm ;
And tuneful voices mingled there,
  To wake the morning Psalm.

It was a sacred spot to me,
  The tranquil groves among,
Where song-birds flit from tree to tree,
  And trill their May-day song.

And when the aged pastor's feet
  Were heard along the aisle,
His loving flock would turn to meet
  His kindly beaming smile.

His head with silver locks was crown'd,
  His eye with age was dim ;
But with a voice of heavenly sound,
  He gave the opening hymn.

And when he spake, his accents calm
  A holy hope express'd ;
To suffering pilgrims it was balm,
  And to the weary rest.

And till the last each listening ear
  His every utterance heard ;
The aged hearts felt heaven near,
  The young with fervour stirr'd.

With grateful minds his flock receiv'd
  His blessing at the close ;
And then from all vain fears reliev'd,
  With strengthen'd hearts they rose.

But now no more shall they behold
  Their guide so true and brave ;
He sleeps in peace, the pastor old,
  Within his quiet grave.

Dilston Hall.

THE shades of tranquil evening creep
    Round Dilston's old and crumbling hall;
The song-birds in their bowers sleep,
    Lull'd by the restless waterfall.

Round Dilston Hall the charms of spring
    In sweet perfection are displayed;
The stately trees their shadows fling
    On winding path and verdant glade.

And birds of brightest plumage make
    Their dwellings in the dell so deep;
The streams reverberant echoes wake
    Among the crags that crown the steep.

From Dilston Hall the traveller sees
    Tyne's fertile vale extending wide,
With Sandhoe 'mid ancestral trees,
    That variegate the green hill-side.

Oh, what a scene for tranquil thought,
    With nature's choicest beauties near,
To piteous mourn the hapless lot
    Of one who lived admired here.

The brave young Earl, his noble name
    Doth still a grateful reverence find,
Whose only fault deserv'd no blame—
    The offspring of a generous mind.

Ill-omen'd day that saw him ride
   From Dilston's beautiful domain,
His staunch retainers by his side,
   To aid his Prince's project vain.

And many a prayer would go with him,
   From hearts his bounty often cheer'd;
And eyes would scan the distance dim,
   In dread suspense till he appear'd.

But never more his steed, elate,
   To Dilston Hall its master bore;
His vassals at the open gate,
   Their lord shall welcome nevermore.

For by the headsman's stroke he fell,
   Of all Northumbria the pride;
And fathers still their children tell
   How noble Derwentwater died.

NOTE.—Dilston Hall was the residence of James, Earl of Derwentwater,
who was executed on Tower-hill, February 23rd, 1716, for aiding the cause of
Charles Stuart. For a particular account of the life and character of this amiable
but unfortunate nobleman, the reader is referred to a very interesting work on
the " Historical and Traditionary Records of Hexham and its neighbourhood,"
which will shortly be published by my talented friend, Mr. P. Davidson, of
Hexham.

The Countess of Derwentwater's Lament.

THEY hae re't his life wi' bluidy hands;—
 I sit an' pine in lanesome dolour;
My een are springs o' scalding tears,
 That frae my cheek hae wash'd the colour.

My lord was ane o' the goodliest men
 That ever own'd leal-hearted lady;
His form was made i' the shapliest mould,
 Wi' luve-bricht een, and cheek sae ruddy.

But fix'd and cauld are his luve-bricht e'en,
 And like the snaw his cheek sae ruddy;
His locks that were o' the silken sheen
 Lie matted owre his forehead bluidy.

The head that lay on my luving breast,
 By villain hands is gash'd and gory;—
Ye Tynedale faihers tell your sons
 Hoo foully fell your chiefest glory.

The cotter's wife sits doon by the Tyne,
 She has nae gift o' land or money;
She lulls her bairn wi' a sweet wee sang,
 That smiles i' her face sae winsome bonny.

I'll lull my bairn wi' a sarg o' bluid,
 I'll tell him a tale o' strife and slaughter;
Weapons o' war shall his playthings be,
 Till he smite the faes o' Derwentwater.

Futurity.

I STOOD before the throne of Night,
  Who sat in sable thrones bedight,
    That shroud her regal face ;
I heard her mystic voices rise,
And saw her myriad burning eyes,
    That pierce the realms of space.

Within her courts dim shadows stirr'd,
And only whispering echoes heard
    Among her spacious halls ;
And through the gloom pale phantoms stole :
While inspiration on my soul,
    Like spirit-music falls.

There is a mystery in the night,
Which lures my soul on upward flight,
    Of earthly trammels rid.
Oh mystery, pervading all,
The future lies beneath thy pall
    From man's weak vision hid.

Oh ! I would break the narrow bound,
Wherein all human skill is found,
    And by some secret spell
Would read the inmost mind of man,
Yea, dark Futurity would scan,
    The world's events foretel.

The sage with all his mighty lore,
To-morrow's course can ne'er explore,
   To-morrow's deeds relate.
Will nature's wondrous voice be woke.
To deign response, while I invoke,
   To learn the will of Fate ?

Ye winds, that wander everywhere,
Along the viewless fields of air,
   And through the forest's gloom;
I hear your mingled voices near;
Can ye not whisper in my ear
   Aught of the time to come ?

Ye clouds, of many a regal hue,
That soar in heaven's unfathom'd blue.
   Where potent spirits dwell ;
As o'er your crests their wings are furl'd,
The secrets of another world
   Have ye not heard them tell ?

Ye mountains, in your hollow caves
The foul night-demon ceaseless raves,
   And gibbering sprites are heard ;
Ye echo to the thunder's roar;
But of the storms that loom before
   Can ye not give me word?

Ye rivers, murmuring to the coast,
Grand as the tread of armed host,
   Or stir of angel's wing ;

Ye roll in majesty and state ;
But of my dim hereafter fate
   Can ye no tidings bring ?

Ye stars, that whirl through endless space,
Among your signs I fail to trace
   My destiny reveal'd,
In Nature's voice or midnight dreams;
And from all human ken it seems
   Futurity is seal'd.

I heard a whisper'd echo nigh,—
" O puny mortal ! cease to pry
   For knowledge long forbid ;
'Tis well for thee, when every day
Brings heavier storms to cloud thy way,
   Thy future fate is hid.

" Walk thou erect in duty's path,
So to avert the doom of wrath,
   For wilful errors given ;
Speak peace to all, or friends or foes,
Fear not the worst of earthly woes,
   But place thy trust in heaven."

Queen Margaret's Flight.

WITH deadly hate, by Devil's stream,
　　The rival Roses warr'd;
The thirsty blades aloft did gleam,
　　And groans of death were heard.

Two armies met on Devil's banks,
　　To urge a kindred claim;
And fiercely fought the hostile ranks,
　　And close the strife became.

The white rose triumphs o'er the red,
　　Which lies, all tarni.h'd, prone;
And Henry from the battle fled,
　　On nimble steed, alone.

The high-soul'd Margaret, with her son,
　　Had left the bloody scene;
To cheer her fallen fate was none,
　　And lonesome felt the queen.

The shouts of victory were behind,
　　The gloomy woods before;
Where shall the twain a refuge find
　　From foes that press them sore?

On, on, through copse and craggy dell,
　　By rugged paths they strove,
Until the shades of twilight fell,
　　And fill'd each leafy grove.

When sudden at her front appear'd
    A band of robbers rude,
Who own'd no law, nor monarch fear'd,
    Amid that solitude.

They stript her of her jewels, while
    She trembled sore afraid;
But, as they clamour'd o'er the spoil,
    Once more escape she made.

She wander'd mid the forest's gloom,
    In sad, despairing plight;
For darker shades than fill the tomb,
    Hung o'er the face of night.

Nor long she'd left the ruffian band,
    Still clamouring o'er their prey,
Until a voice made rude demand,
    " Who is it comes this way?"

One stood before her, who did seem
    Of stalwart, manly frame;
And Margaret, in her last extreme,
    Gave utterance to her name.

"And here, entrusted to thy care,
    Behold thy prince"! she said.
" Lady, with dearest life, I swear
    To give my utmost aid.

" For base indeed, my soul had been—
    Devoid of feelings just,
If to a pleading, fallen queen
    I should betray my trust."

Then through the forest paths he led,
    And down a craggy steep;
They cross'd a streamlet's narrow bed,
    Within the dell so deep.

He show'd a cavern's mouth, and said,
    "Here ye may safely rest;
Though rude the dwelling I have made,
    Yet none shall ye molest."

With grateful hearts they gladly shared
    His safe, though mean abode,
Where store of comforts were prepared,
    Which freely he bestow'd.

Here, in the robber's cave she stayed
    Till all pursuit was past;
And, by secure means conveyed,
    She reach'd her kin at last.

The spot is shown, which to a queen
    Its gloomy shelter gave;
And strangers visit oft the scene,
    To view "Queen Margaret's Cave."

NOTE.—History is uncertain as to the exact spot where the Battle of Hexham was fought, which for a time decided the important contest between the rival Houses of York and Lancaster, but it is generally admitted to have been some where near the Devil's Water. The "Guard's Lonning" at Dipton Mill has undoubtedly received its name from associations with the battle. The farm house of "Queen's Letch" is supposed to stand near the spot where Queen Margaret met the robber, who conducted her to the cave, where she found a safe retreat until, at a fitting opportunity, she escaped into Scotland.

The "Queen's Cave" is situated in a very picturesque dell, opposite the farm house of Bleakhill. It is now ruinous, but gives evidence of having been once divided into two compartments; the queen resided in the smaller, and interior one with her son, guarded by the robber.

Reminiscences of an Old Farmer.

His mind is as dark
    As a cave underground :
All the soul that he has
    In his cash-box is found.
He values his self
    By his work like a horse,
He values his friend
    By the length of his purse.

WHAT changes there hes been! sin' aw can meynd lang syne,
    There was ne steam machines, ne railway up the Tyne;
We thrash'd wor corn wuv sticks—a slow and tedious way;
But thor machine. knock off twe hundred bouls a day.
When coorn cam forrit fast, it gav' us muckle grief,
For 'twas cutten up wi' heuks, and gether'd wi' the neif;
Aw yence had hoaf me crop o' battered wi' the wuud,
'Twas stanniu' rotten reype, ne wark-foak cood be fuud;—
Says aw. " thoo muckle de'il, thaw varra warstest blow,
Sin thoo's teyn away the coorn, thoo may teyk the stree an oa."

Thame days the sarviu' lads was train'd to de yen's biddin';
The wummin foak fill'd muck, an' lasses turn'd the midden;
Aw was king amang the heynds, an' maister 'mang the weyves;
Aw cood gar the geypin lads work oot their varra leyves,
But noo they gan ta skeul, au' lairn se much conceit,
They grummle at their wark, and grunt aboot their meat,
On beef an' groser dumplings they varra fain wad feed,
Wi' tea. by George ! o' Sundays, an' butter on their breid.
What dis a plewman want wi' skeulin, aw wad ken ?
If he can work his wark, an' coont as far as ten;
But he mun read the papers leyke ony uther squire;
'Twad leuk mair tiv his mense ta gau an' muck the byre.

What canny little weyges we used ta hae ta pay !
Now men 'ill hardly chop under hoaf-a-croon a day;
An' yit they pleen o' hunger if it cums a week o' wet;
Aw wonder what they de wuv oa the brass they get ?
But they gan ta sic expense wi' lairnin' bairns their letters,
An' gettin' Sunday claes leyke ony o' their betters;
When aw was young they teuk a lang way better plan,
The bairns was put ta wark as seun as they could gan,
An' kept i' workin' order, lantern-jaw'd an' lean,
Wi' crowdies tweyce a day, and barley-breid atween.
The boudagers pull'd turnips for fower-pence a day,
Wuv stree ropes round their legs ta keep the suaw away;
An' weel aw gar'd them work, till they could'nt gan or stand.
Then wark wus varra scarce, we cood keep the upper-hand.

Aw had a man neym'd Hodge, a doonreet de'il for wark,—
Aw think aw see him noo, wuv his patch'd and dorty sark.
Across the meidow rigs his scythe wad foremost gan,
An' in the midden-steed he was a mighty man;
Yen season, we war thrang, aw tried maw faiv'reet dodge,
Aw gat a stoot young chep ta mow alang wuv Hodge.
" An' noo," says aw, " maw lads, let's see which o' ye's best;"
Sae hard on Hodge's heels the stoot young fellow prest;
An' sic a breadth o' grund, as aw that day gat deun,
Was nivver deun afore, an' nivver will ageyn.
Hodge went ta bed that neet, but nivver ris ne mair,
Next day he kick'd the bucket, after grainin' lang an' sair:
Aw meynd the teym first-rate, we war cairtin' in the hay.
The best naig ivver aw had, gat leym'd that varra day;
An' efter sic a loss aw did'nt feel quite happy,—
They war strang an' willin' workers, beuth Hodge an' poor
　　o'd Cappy

But aw's gettin' o'd mesel, maw turn 'll cum ta gan,
Aw's thankful that aw've been a money-meykin' man;
Aw started off wi little, but aw 've getten plenty noo;
Maw sons they shape ta follow maw varra footsteps throo,
Aw tell them hoo ta gaird their troosers-pocket neuks,
They nivver tease their brains wuv readin' silly beuks.
Maw beuk-shelf ho'ds a Beyble, an' some o'd almanacks,
" Robin Burns's Poems" an' three or fower trac's.
Aw get the "Hue an' Cry," ta see the market news;
An' clubs in wi' me neighbors ta pay the quarter dues.
Aw'll not incourish beggars ta cum an' pester me,
Maw "Bleezer" varra seun gars the raggymuffins flee;—
Sae mony poor foaks meyke a vast expense an bother,
When they becum hard up can't they leeve o' yen anuther.
Aw ailwus gan o' Sundays ta hear a bit o' prayer,
An' when they beelt the Cheppel' aw' gav' a guddish share ;
The minister's maw freend, ta Hivven aw'll shure gan;
Not leykely they'll bar oot a much respectect man.

Rodulf the Riever.

PART 1.

FIERCE Rodulf dwelt in his tower strong,
    The head of a riever band,
Who up and down, by farm and town,
    Did harry all the land.

They brought the beeves and good milch kine
  That grazed in Teviot's dale;
And the portly abbot he lost his wine,
  And the burgher miss'd his ale.

O, merrily lived the riever band
  In wassail every day;
By night they rode on the Scottish land,
  And deftly choose their prey.

There lived a knight, war-worn and grey,
  In his castle by the stream;
And he had a daughter fair as the day,
  And sweet as love's first dream.

Rodulf by chance sweet Eveline spied,
  As like a wood-nymph fair,
She wandered by the river side
  To breathe the summer air.

The maid was beauteous to behold;
  Fresh as the morn her face;
Her form was shaped in beauty's mould,
  And full of angel grace.

And Rodulf's heart was fired with love,
  But must his suit refrain;
His rugged mien would fright the dove
  Back to her bower again.

He watched her as she tripped along
  Beneath the forest's shade;
The song-birds trill'd their sweetest song
  To charm the beauteous maid.

Then back again to his tower he hied,
　　While passion tost his soul;
And the eager flame in his heart became
　　So fierce, beyond control.

But he brooded dark on baneful schemes,
　　As brews the winter storm;
And his lurid eye shot fiery gleams,
　　As fancy traced her form.

Fair Eveline's father sat at his board,
　　Where feasted all who came:
One knocked at his gate who craved a word
　　In the riever Rodulf's name.

"What kind of message, varlet, dare
　　That robber send to me."
"'Tis that he would take thy daughter fair,
　　His loving bride to be."

Then fury glared from his haughty eye,
　　And he said to his vassals twain,
"Let that daring wretch have short reply,
　　Root out his tongue profane,

"And send him back to his hell-born chief,
　　To show him a lesson dread;
Let him read with fear my answer brief
　　In his varlet's tongueless head."

Then Rodulf, when the man return'd,
　　Did rave both loud and long,
To see his loathsome offer scorn'd,
　　And his serf without a tongue.

"Arm! arm!" he cried, "my merry men all,
   For I swear by the cross divine,
That old Sir Guy this night shall die,
   And his daughter yet be mine."

Fair Eveline sat in her bower alone,
   Heart-heavy and forlorn;
Her lover long to the wars had gone,
   And she waited his return.

Sir Edmund was a goodly knight,
   Of lineage high he came;
And the sword he wore in his country's right.
   Had won him wealth and fame.

And Eveline's maiden heart did cling
   To Edmund in the war;
But love, I wis, is a weary thing,
   When the loved one is afar.

And longing now for his quick return,
   She sits in her bower alone;
The twilight shades are downward borne:
   Another day has flown.

Her bright eyes scan the forest trees,
   That fill the glen below;
She, startled, 'mid their umbrage sees
   Dark forms move to and fro.

Sudden the riever's charge doth sound,
   Is heard the answering yell ;
And his savage troopers start around,
   Like demons loosed from hell.

They force the castle's massy gate,
　　In vain the guard oppose,
Too feeble all against the hate
　　Which nerves their ruthless foes.

Sir Guy, whose ears the stirring peal
　　Of murderous strife assail'd,
He grasped his sword of the trusty steel,
　　Which never in battle fail'd.

But when the open court he gain'd,
　　Appall'd apace he stood;
His men lay prone on the pavement stain'd
　　And slippery with their blood.

"Old tiger, yield!" cried the riever chief,
　　"Till my followers sack thy lair;
For me, my errand is plain and brief,
　　I come for thy daughter fair."

"Vile robber, never ! though frail with eld,
　　Thy power I still defy;"
And his sword with firmer grasp was held,
　　As eager to do or die.

"Nor will my daughter so young and fair,
　　To thy foul embraces yield;"—
And his weapon rang, with a sudden clang,
　　On Rodulf's brazen shield.

Instant by many a ruffian arm
　　The brave old knight was smote;
Fierce Rodulf leapt on his fallen form,
　　And gashed his panting throat.

"Now die," he said, "while my followers bold
　　Do quaff thy choicest wine;
But the fairest gem within thy hold—
　　Thy daughter—she is mine."

Fair Eveline, trembling, in her bower,
　　The sudden conflict heard;
She saw the rievers force the tower,
　　And murder all the guard.

But when beneath o'erwhelming arms
　　Her sire was crush'd to earth,
Her heart was filled with sore alarms,
　　And pale, she issued forth.

There lay the knight, so good and brave.
　　Who loved his daughter fair;
And wild she wept, and loud did rave,
　　And tore her shining hair.

She raised from earth his bleeding head:
　　He feebly turned his eye;
A moment more, and his soul had fled
　　Above with a parting sigh.

'Tis fearful to gaze on a form we love
　　In the quiet sleep of death,
When the glowing eyes have ceased to move,
　　And the warm lips yield no breath.

More fearful still, when by ruthless hands
　　The life beloved is ta'en,
And the warm red blood, in a wasteful flood,
　　The cold, cold ground doth stain.

So gentle Eveline's desolate heart
　　Sank low with grief oppress'd,
Till a flood of scalding tears did start,
　　To ease her labouring breast.

Said Rodulf, " Spare thy beauteous eyes,
　　Though prone upon the ground,
In loathful death thy sire lies,
　　Thou hast a lover found."

She turned upon the black-browed chief
　　With a scornful quick reply;
Yet all too weak the hate to wreak
　　That shone in her angry eye.

" Go, demons, bear my withering curse,—
　　Thou and thy ruffian crew;
Let the scathing pains of chill remorse
　　Your hateful paths pursue.

" Could ye not spare his hoary eld
　　Your vengeance dark and fierce ?
O that I were a thousand swords,
　　Your wolfish hearts to pierce !

" But there is one, upon whose arm
　　For vengeance I rely,—
A noble knight, before whose might
　　Thy puny strength will die."

" Ha, is it so," dark Rodulf said,
　　" Who'er thy lord may be,
Until he comes, my bonny maid,
　　Thou must content with me.

" Now sack this den, my merry men,
    And let the red flames burn;
And, laden, we will ride agen,
    To wassail on the morn."

PART II.

Sir Edmund, now the wars were o'er,
    Made haste his love to greet ;
And honours high, and wealth he bore,
    To lay beneath her feet.

And many a weary day they rode,
    His followers staunch and he,
To reach his lady-love's abode,
    Her welcome smile to see.

And ever would active fancy trace
    Her well remembered charms ;
He long'd for the kiss and the kind embrace—
    The clasp of her loving arms.

And ever in thought he heard her speak
    In the passing zephyr's sigh;
He saw the glow on her maiden cheek,
    And the light in her angel eye.

At length in sight of her bower he came,
    As the twilight shadows fall ;
But little he wist that blood and flame
    Was filling her father's hall.

Ere long through night's fast gathering shade,
   He saw with wild amaze,
The red flames rise to the lurid skies,
   The castle all ablaze.

He spurr'd his steed with mad alarm,—
   " Now forward, every one ;
I wot there is some cruel harm
   To lady Eveline done."

Then onward like the sweeping Nile,
   They rushed in mad career ;
Till in the strait of a deep defile,
   Did Rodulf's band appear.

Their leader bore the beauteous maid
   Before him on his steed ;
On Edmund's name she called for aid,
   Who came with whirlwind speed.

Dark Rodulf wheel'd his charger back,
   His dear-won gem to save ;
Leaving his men to stand the shock
   Sir Edmund's onset gave.

On came the knight; in his strong right hand
   His brandish'd sword did blaze;
He cleft his way through the riever band
   Like sunburst through the haze.

His followers all like warriors brave,
   The sturdy rievers fought;
But he had an angel's life to save,
   And a demon's blood he sought.

On, on, by love and hatred stirr'd,
    The trail he did pursue;
And ever his Eveline's voice he heard,
    As aye he closer drew.

The pall of night hung thickly round;
    The pale moon hid her face ;
The woods were wrapt in gloom profound ;
    Yet keener grew the chase.

Still Rodulf clasped the beauteous maid
    Within his rude embrace ;
And still his steed, with thundering speed,
    Kept foremost in the race.

Yet closer, closer, drew the knight,
    And press'd the riever sore ;
"Oh, save me," Eveline cried, "and I
    Am thine for evermore."

Rodulf, with fear and jealous hate,
    His coming foe did see ;
" Fair maid," said he, " accept thy fate,
    For his thou shalt not be."

Then deep in her gentle breast he sheath'd
    His dagger keen and bright ;
A sweet farewell and a prayer she breath'd
    For her good and gallant knight.

And prone on earth, the lovely maid
    In death's embrace did bleed ;
And deep in the forest's dismal shade
    Did Rodulf urge his steed.

Sir Edmund yields the fearful chase,
    By Eveline's form to stay ;
He check'd his courser's fiery pace,
    And halted where she lay.

But gone was the glow of life that shone
    On her pure cheek and brow ;
And the heart that beat for him alone,
    Was still and pulseless now.

He raised the beauteous form which lay
    In death prostrated low ;
The sweet young life had oozed away,
    In a wasteful crimson flow.

Oh, then he raised the loud lament,
    And grief's despairing moan ;
His heart with many a pang was rent,
    For the love of his life was gone.

But he remembered evermore
    Dark Rodulf's hellish art ;
And by many a sacred oath he swore
    To tear his wolfish heart.

But the heart that knew no fear before,
    Became a desolate blank ;
His heaven, his Eveline, was no more,
    And his soul despairing sank.

The chilly waves of dark despond
    O'erwhelmed his senses all ;
And crush'd by sorrow's weight he swoon'd,
    And prone to earth did fall.

'Tis sad to see the generous mien
　　Beneath despair's dark cloud ;
'Tis sad to see the genial heart
　　By heavy sorrow bow'd.

Dark Rodulf left his panting steed
　　To roam the glade alone ;
And turn'd to view the hellish deed
　　His ruthless hand had done.

And hid behind a shadowy tree,
　　It made his heart rejoice,
Sir Edmund's writhing grief to see,
　　To hear his wailing voice.

But jealous hate his brow did cloud,
　　Dark as the winter storm,
When he heard Sir Edmund's threatenings loud,
　　For he feared his mighty arm.

He saw the strong man faint away
　　'Neath sorrow's crushing weight ;
His stalwart form insensate lay,
　　Which sooth'd the riever's hate.

Then tiger-like, he closer crept,
　　His dagger drew again,
And fierce on Edmund's throat he leapt,
　　And cleft his heart in twain.

Then with a loud exultant shout
　　He sheathed his gory knife ;
" Thus ever," he cried, " my art shall flout
　　Their aims who seek my life."

He cross'd his steed of the ebon-black,
   His face did homeward turn;
But I wot he'll ride on a weary track,
   Before he meets the morn.

Soft was the breath of the summer night,
   And calm as an infant's rest;
But the canker and curse of a soul's remorse
   Corrodes his tortured breast.

The mournful wind like a demon's hiss,
   Would startle his guilty ear;
And pleading eyes with a sad reproach,
   In his ghastly face would peer.

He urged his steed to a headlong pace,
   To flee each horrent sight;
But ever would follow the frowning face
   Of the newly murdered knight.

And ever would Eveline's dying sigh
   On the solemn night-breeze come;
And onward, away his steed did fly,
   To bear him quick to his doom.

Away, like the sky-rack borne by the wind,
   To the distant sounding shore;
Away, with the vengeful foe behind,
   And the meed of death before.

Away to the edge of the towering steep,
   On the distant sounding shore;
Below, the waters are dark and deep,
   Where the angry eddies roar.

The fiery courser spurns the steep,
   That stands on the sounding shore;
And horse and rider dive in the deep,
   Which clasps them evermore.

     *   *   *   *

By sulphurous wings the gloom was stirr'd
   Along the seething deep;
A demon's mocking laugh was heard
   Beyond the frowning steep.

At length the herald chanticleer
   Announc'd Aurora nigh;
Her path all radiant did appear,
   Along the eastern sky.

The gloomy shades of night did flee
   Before her golden ray;
The glowing earth and glittering sea,
   Smiled welcome to the day.

I Will.

DESPAIR not, O my panting soul !
  By ceaseless struggles worn ;
The clouds of fate will backward roll,
  The sunshine will return.
Though toilsome oft my path has been,
  And cares beset me still,
Yet will I reach the hills of green,
  Where summer smiles—*I will.*

In dark obscurity I lay,
  Unworthy men's esteem ;
I saw the fluttering motes that play
  In golden plenty's beam.
The worldling weak may fume and fret,
  His dearling purse to fill ;
I'll leave a name of honour yet
  Shall his outlive—*I will.*

Up in the might of manhood's prime,
  In light of genius go ;
Write truths upon the page of time,
  That shall eternal glow.
Though servile chains and penury bind
  The frame to hardship still,
I'll soar in spirit unconfin'd
  Beyond earth's bound—*I will.*

The empty things that walk the earth
    With self-complacent stride,
By Fortune cherish'd from their birth,
    How swells their mien with pride!
Although I bear the worldling's scoff,
    And cares impede me still,
I'll throw the vulgar trammels off
    That bind my thoughts—*I will.*

Despair not, then, O yearning heart,
    But rise in courage strong,
Though I have neither lot nor part
    With yonder gaudy throng.
Away with every warping fear,
    Press onward, upward still;
I'll win a name that men shall hear
    With loud acclaim—I WILL.

Hexham Fell.

DID you ever stray on Hexham Fell,
    On a quiet eve in the month of May?
When the wee birds sang in the leafy dell,
    A farewell hymn to the dying day.

Did you mark the quiet town below,
    With its fringe of trees and gardens green ?
Did you see where the stately Tyne doth flow,
    With a pleasing murmur through the scene ?

And oh, did you hear the Abbey bells
    Ring sweetly forth from the towering fane ?
Whose music filled the leafy dells,
    And echoed back from the hills again.

We love the Abbey ; its grandeur sage
    The deeds of the mighty past recalls ;
Our fathers in many a bygone age,
    Have worshipp'd within its hoary walls.

Oh, sweet is the view from Hexham Fell,
    With its gorgeous woods and fields of green :
The enamell'd hills that backwards swell,
    And the sheeny river that rolls between.

In Hexham town are maidens fair,
    With the liquid voice and the laughing eye,
To solace man in his hour of care,
    And charm the grief that ventures nigh.

My native scenes I would not leave,
    For I love their tranquil beauty well ;
And I love to sit on a summer eve,
    'Mid the charms they yield, on Hexham Fell.

" Bring, oh, bring."

BRING, oh, bring me quickly here
　　A pound of steaks and a pint of beer ;
My heart is sad as sad can be,
For the charming widow has jilted me.

I had no peace when she was nigh,
For mischief lurk'd in her laughing eye ;
Yet I could not, could not keep away,
Her smile would haunt me night and day.

Her voice could charm like a song of glee ;
But, oh, her lips, how they tempted me !
I'd leave my glass of the ruby wine,
For a single touch of her lips divine.

Like a daffodilly I pined away,
A-thinking about her every day;
Till one fine night, just after tea,
I asked her plump would she marry me.

She seal'd me up with her answer brief,
It cool'd my heart like a cabbage leaf ;
I'll hang my harp on a gooseberry tree,
And away to the Fenian wars I'll flee.

But, no—I'll stay, and the girls I'll court,
'Twill vex my charmer to see the sport ;
For I can reckon her up to a T,
The charming widow that jilted me.

Blithe Isabel.

OH! beauty still lingers to gladden the earth,
And harmony springs with rejoicing and mirth,
And love has a power the people to sway,
For hope ever lives in its quickening ray ;
And a bonnie young flower doth bloom on the fell,
The pride of the garden, the blithe Isabel.

Oh! she's sweet as the breath of the new-open'd rose,
And fresh as the morn when the summer wind blows,
She is fresh, she is fair as the sun-radiance cast
On the luminous earth when the rain-cloud hath past;
Her voice hath a music whose charm doth excel
The song-birds in sweetness, the blithe Isabel.

Where the fairest assemble she reigns the chief star,
And lovers crowd round her, or worship afar ;
Oh, merriment swims in her clear speaking eye,
And wit gives a grace to each sprightly reply ;
Yet her heart is unconquer'd though leaguer'd right well.
She will yield it to none, will the blithe Isabel.

I met her at eve, as she came up the hill,
And told her how love was tormenting me still,
How each moment of life at her service should be,
If she'd deign the sweet smile of affection on me ;—
"Indeed, it's a sorrowful tale that you tell ;
Could I help you, I would," laugh'd the blithe Isabel.

The Hills of the North.

INSCRIBED TO MR. THOMAS HARLE, JUN., CHRISTCHURCH,
NEW ZEALAND.

DEAR friend of my youth, in the morning of life,
When our hearts were untouch'd by its tumult and strife:
When our feelings were fresh as the dew at the dawn,
And doubt and deceit in our bosoms unknown;
Then the pathway before us with promise was gilt,
And castles of air in the future were built;
Then true-love and friendship gave beauty to earth,
And happy we strayed on the hills of the North.

We have wander'd together by valley and hill,
Like birds of the mountain that soar at their will;
We have stood side by side on the high mountain-crest,
When the day-king had passed through the gates of the west;
The lark, heaven's songster, did carol in glee,
And our souls with its music would bound to be free;
As the eagle doth spurn the base trammels of earth,
Our hearts did exult on the hills of the North.

We have read the deep lines of the bard o'er and o'er,
And mused how he gather'd such beautiful lore;
How virtue was succour'd, how punish'd was crime
By the heroes that lived in the good olden time.

And our hearts would be kindled with emulous fire,
And burn with an eager exalted desire;
Like the eagle, whose wing the swift arrow doth pierce,
Impotent must battle with enemies fierce.

We loved the charms which the summer-time yields,
The green walls of forest, the flower-starred fields;
We would gaze on their beauty enraptured for ever,
The sun-gilded hills, and the bright gleaming river.
We loved the music the summer-time brings,
When down in the dell the nightingale sings;
And the leaf-shaded streamlets that tinkle along,
Their cadence would add to its beautiful song.

We have roamed on the hills in the bleak winter night,
And watch'd the grey plovers whirl round in their flight;
And ever their wail would be heard as they past,
To join with shrill cadence the roar of the blast.
On the far mountain summit the storm king did ride,
And dark were the garments in which he did pride;
And sombre his mien, and his voice echo'd far,
Like the tread of an army when marching to war.

O, sweet dream of childhood, that e'er it should end!
That the world's weary cares should the bright spirit bend:
And the soul that would soar to catch glimpses of heaven.
To silence and torpor by hardship be driven.
But the dark days appeared, the reality came,
And damp'd with its horror the soul's eager flame;
We must bend to the fetters, or wandering forth,
Bid a lasting farewell to the hills of the North.

Thou didst manfully onward life's journey pursue,—
From thee even labour a dignity drew;
In the world's eager battle thou didst overcome,
And a far foreign country has furnish'd thy home;
There with acres thy own thou canst labour at will,
And the wealth-yielding soil for thy own profit till;
The marks of dependence are gone from thy mien,
And plenty and peace in thy dwelling is seen.

For me, I embark'd on the torrent of life,
Unable to bear with its wearisome strife;
It irks me to guard against each puny wave—
To seize each advantage my neighbour should have;
It rankles my heart and it weighs on my soul
To ask of my fellow for labour's poor dole;
Wealth's gold-gilded bark glided smoothly away,
But troubled the waves where desponding I lay.

I sail'd with the current, and never took heed
Of the manifold dangers to which it should lead;
I left the calm scenes of my boyhood behind,
In the tumult of life consolation to find;
I sought for oblivion in scenes that were low,
Where the loud laugh was heard, and the mirth-cup did flow;
How deeply degraded, how fallen was I!
I lived without thought, without thought meant to die.

O, friend of my childhood, hadst thou but been near,
To check the wild force of my heedless career;
Yet often the shield of thy influence came,
To guard me from acts that accumulate shame.

When wasted with fever, till hope was no more,
I lay through long months on a far-distant shore,
A kind voice of comfort came o'er the wide sea,
Which spoke to my lone heart of home and of thee.

And now, all unscath'd, the dread ordeal I've pass'd,
And a portion of peace has been doled me at last;
I sit 'mid the scenes where we loved to stray,
Where my heart still would linger when far, far away.
The home-scenes of yore, they are beautiful still,—
The sweet scented vale, and the many hued-hill;—
Oh, Nature has beauties all over the earth,
But none can me charm like the hills of the North.

May peace be thy portion, dear friend of my youth,
I have witness'd thy worth, I have proven thy truth;
Though we ne'er meet again, my endeavour shall be
That no action of mine is unworthy of thee.
Between us the ocean doth girdle the earth,
We may never clasp hands on the hills of the North;
But when we are rid of this cumbering clay,
Our souls may commingle for ever and aye.